To Blankie and Bus —D.R.

To Pinky and Hop —S.M.

THIS IS A BORZOI BOOK PUBLISHED BY ALFRED A. KNOPF

Text copyright © 2023 by Dan Richards
Jacket art and interior illustrations copyright © 2023 by Shanda McCloskey

All rights reserved. Published in the United States by Alfred A. Knopf, an imprint of
Random House Children's Books, a division of Penguin Random House LLC, New York.

Knopf, Borzoi Books, and the colophon are registered trademarks of Penguin Random House LLC.

Visit us on the Web! rhcbooks.com

Educators and librarians, for a variety of teaching tools, visit us at RHTeachersLibrarians.com

Library of Congress Cataloging-in-Publication Data
Names: Richards, Dan, author. | McCloskey, Shanda, illustrator.
Title: Nubby / by Dan Richards ; illustrations by Shanda McCloskey.
Description: New York : Alfred A. Knopf, [2023] | Audience: Ages 3–7. |
Summary: An overworked stuffed bunny strikes out on a quest for fame and
appreciation, only to realize that home is where he belongs.
Identifiers: LCCN 2022003751 (print) | LCCN 2022003752 (ebook) |
ISBN 978-0-593-38109-0 (hardcover) | ISBN 978-0-593-38110-6 (library binding) |
ISBN 978-0-593-38111-3 (ebook)
Subjects: CYAC: Toys—Fiction. | Rabbits—Fiction. | Love—Fiction. | LCGFT: Picture books.
Classification: LCC PZ7.R3788 Nu 2023 (print) | LCC PZ7.R3788 (ebook) | DDC [E]—dc23

The text of this book is set in 22-point Erstwhile.
The illustrations were created using pencil, Procreate, watercolor, and Photoshop.
Book design by Nicole Gastonguay

MANUFACTURED IN CHINA
10 9 8 7 6 5 4 3 2 1

First Edition

Nubby

By Dan Richards

Illustrated by Shanda McCloskey

Alfred A. Knopf
New York

Nubby was done.

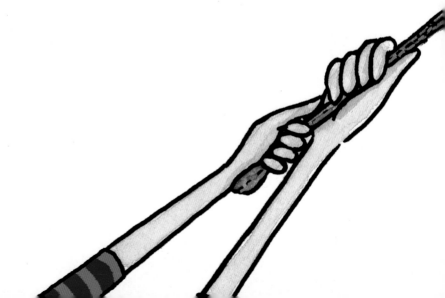

He had been carried, buried, dropped, dragged, torn, worn, chewed on, sat on, and even used as a nose wipe.

Repeatedly.

A bunny can only take so much.
He needed a new beginning.
Somewhere he was appreciated.

That afternoon, while the rest of the house slept, Nubby ventured out into the great wide world.

He had not gone far before he had
a most unexpected meeting.

The resemblance
was uncanny.

Longish ears, poofy tails,
and wrinkly noses.
Friends!
Surely he'd be appreciated here!

But instead of welcoming him, they ignored him.
It was as if they didn't even see him.
His boy would never treat him like that.

His boy would . . .
he couldn't quite put a paw on it.

Oh, well, Nubby told himself.
Something better was bound to come along.
And soon it did.

Nubby landed the starring role in a magic show.
He'd be famous, and then everyone would
adore him.

He just knew it!

But fame can be fickle, and Nubby found himself all alone, back on the street.

Finding someone to appreciate him was hard work.

He longed for a familiar voice, even if sometimes it was whiny and grumpy.

But Nubby was far from home, too far to turn back now.

If popularity and fame weren't the answers, then what could it be?

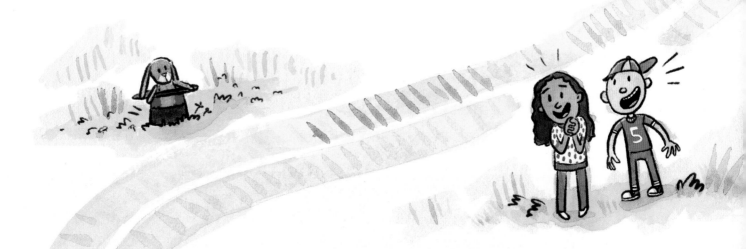

Of course! Why hadn't he thought of it before? He just needed to be . . .

. . . rich!

Then everyone would see how amazing he really was! Nubby set out across oceans and continents, braving all manner of danger searching for treasure.

And he found it! He would be wealthy beyond his wildest dreams, and everyone would *have* to appreciate him. It all seemed so obvious!

Alas, fortunes can be lost
as easily as they can be found.

Nubby lay staring up at the sky.
The pain in his chest cut deep,
deeper than torn cloth
and strewn stuffing.
It went all the way
to the very fabric of his soul.

He missed the old days, laughing and playing with his boy. Remembering brought a sad, fuzzy sort of smile to his face.

Back then, his life had been— What had it been?

SPLAT!

It had been messy and loud and
unruly. But it had also been close,
and unspoken, and . . . *real.*

If only he could go back.
If only it wasn't too late.

And then he made a startling discovery,
a life-changing discovery. A discovery worth all the pain
and loneliness and heartache he had endured.

Nubby pulled himself up, found a ride, and hurried . . .

. . . back home.

Nubby was still carried,
buried, dropped,
dragged, torn, worn,
chewed on, sat on,

and even used as a nose wipe.

But now he barely noticed.

He was too busy being nuzzled, snuggled, cuddled, clutched, bathed, bundled, squeezed, smooched, and utterly adored.

Repeatedly. Just like he'd always been.
Only now he cherished every moment of it.

And that made all the difference.